Terry McManus

Under the Stars

with

Leo-Pard

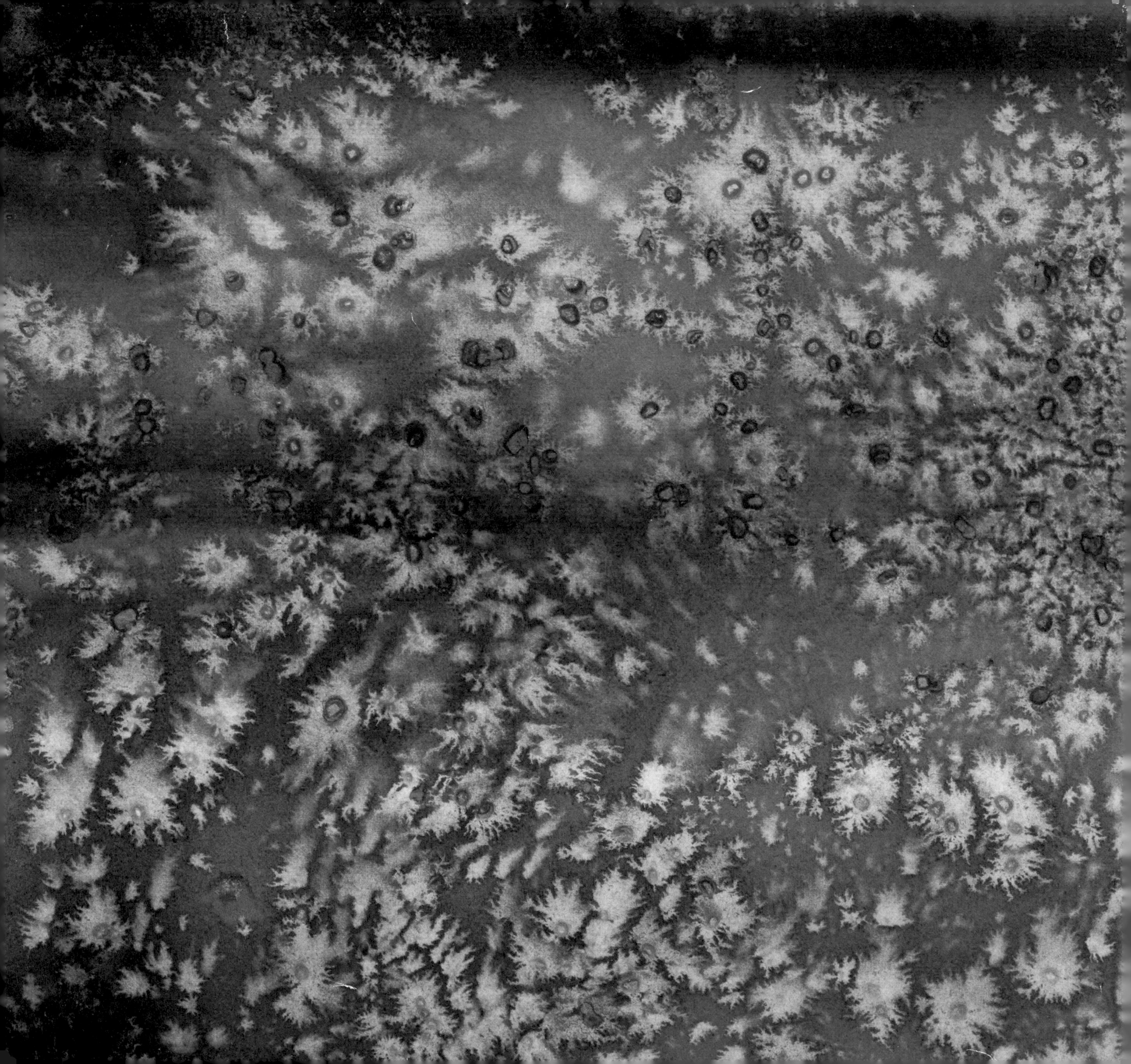

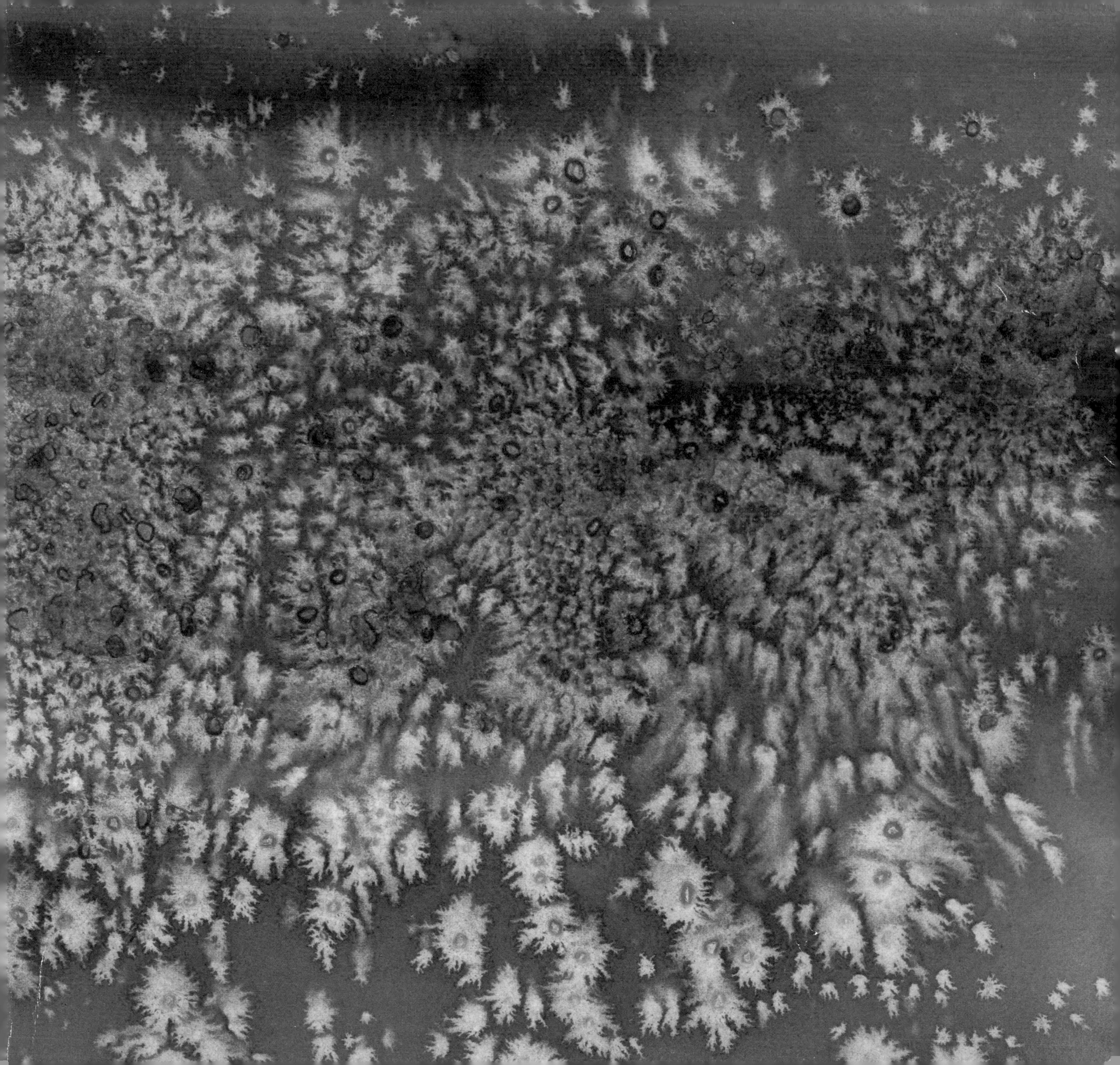

Matador
9 Priory Business Park,
Wistow Road, Kibworth Beauchamp,
Leicestershire. LE8 0RX
Tel: (+44) 116 279 2299
Fax: (+44) 116 279 2277
Email: books@troubador.co.uk
Web: www.troubador.co.uk/matador

ISBN 978 1783062 034

British Library Cataloguing in Publication Data.
A catalogue record for this book is available from the British Library.

Typeset by Troubador Publishing Ltd, Leicester, UK

Matador is an imprint of Troubador Publishing Ltd

Dedicated to my mum, dad and brothers who made me a dreamer,
my patient wife Linda and inspirational children Brogan, Niamh,
Ruan and Will who insisted that I follow those dreams.

My supportive friends Kylia, Don, Stu, Sue and Maggie who helped me
make my dreams come true.

And in memory of Diana Williams the most caring cat person I have ever been
fortunate to have known, sweet dreams Di x

It was the middle of the night but Leo-Pard was wide awake; thoughts drifted in and out of his mind.

I wouldn't exist if it wasn't for this place, nor would any of my friends, he thought to himself.

Tucked away in lush countryside and surrounded by soft, rolling green hills, the morning light appeared over Leo-Pard's home, named My Zoo.

The zoo got its strange name because the owner, the ever-smiling Mr Beamish, was so happy when he finally bought the zoo that he nearly exploded with joy and punched the air, shouting, "It's my zoo now! All mine."

So that's what he called it.

My Zoo

My Zoo rescues and takes care of mistreated animals of all shapes and sizes, whose owners can no longer care for them. It is home to a collection of the world's most weird and wonderful creatures, including:

Cute, not so cute;
scaly, not so scaly;
creepy, not so creepy;
tall, not so tall; and ugly, not so ugly.

It really doesn't matter because My Zoo takes them all.

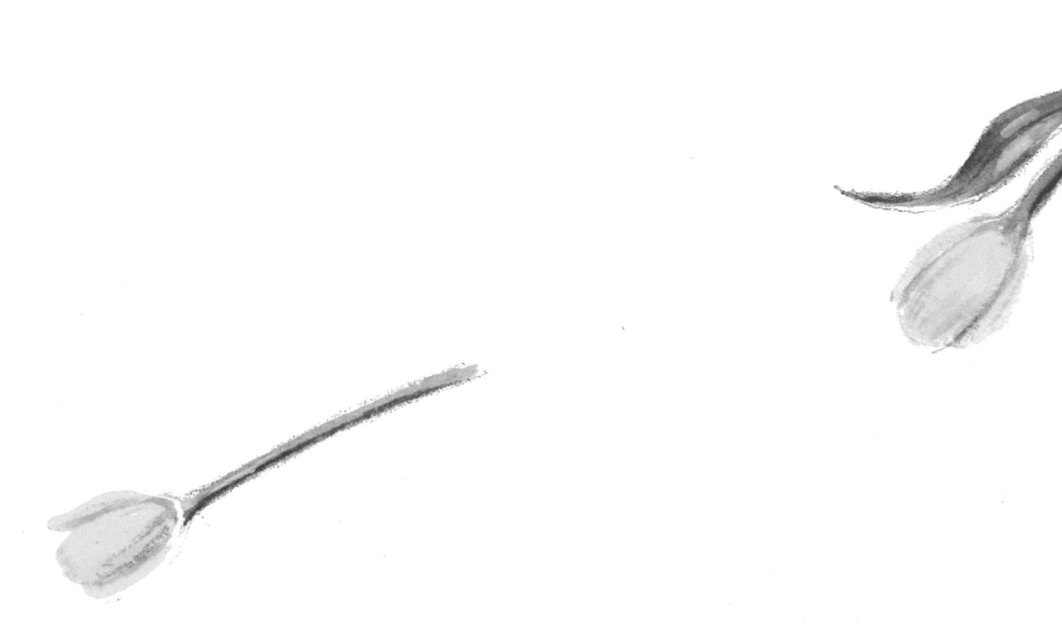

With its caring and friendly staff…

MY ZOO GIFTS
feel yummy sweets.
CRISPS ALL FLAVOURS 20P
Buy one get one FREE ALL SWEETS
Snacks and Treats
Milkshake Banana, Strawberry, Chocolate £1.20
Asserted Lollies
Strawberry Splits
Ice Cream, 75p + £1.50p
Belgian Chocolate, Strawberry, mint, Vanilla.
Cones Single 70p Double with flake £1.50p
Chocolate Brownies 50p each or 6 For £2.50p

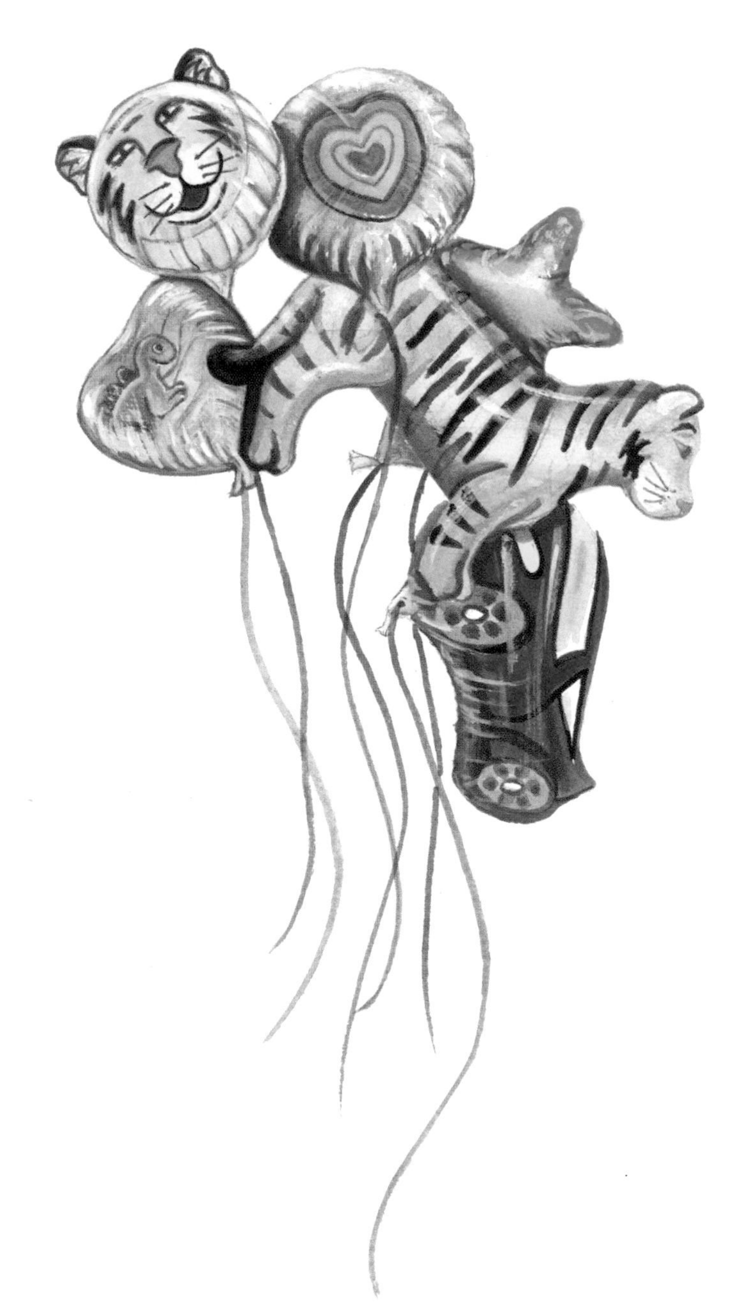

… colourful shops and pleasant surroundings…

… life should have been wonderful. But somehow, the zoo felt like a prison.

What was wrong?

What was missing?

What was it he longed for?

He didn't know the word for it, but it felt like an itch that his claws couldn't reach to scratch.

It felt like an empty inside even though he had just eaten his meaty dinner.

It felt like chilly dampness all around him, though his cage was warm and dry.

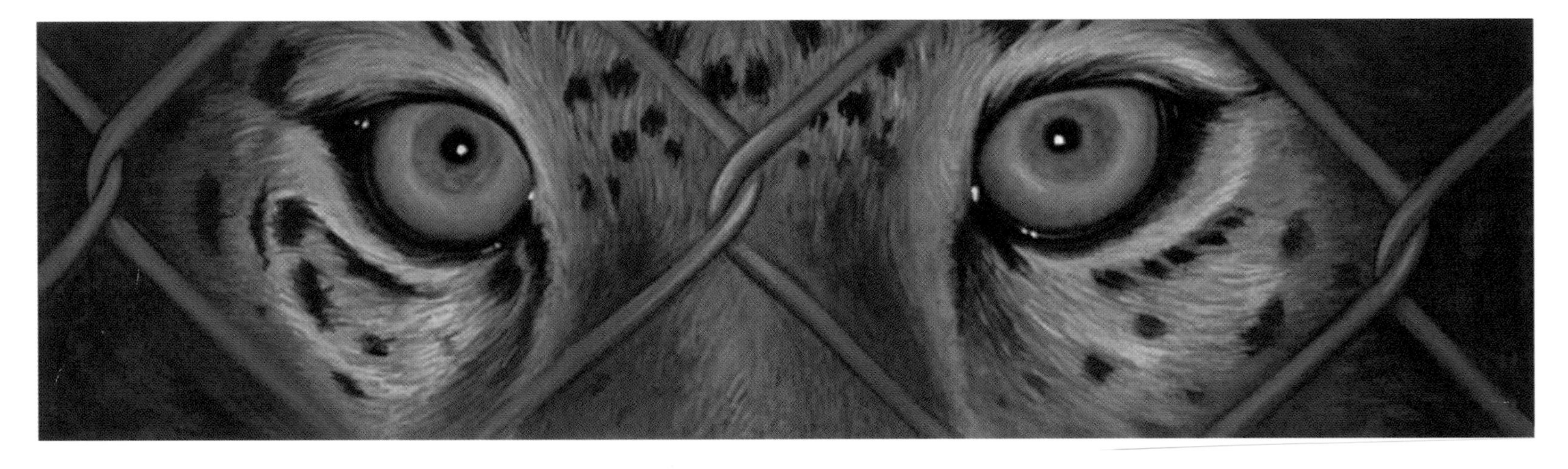

It felt as if no one bothered about him, though his keepers were always kind.

Leo had an idea.

A few days later in the cat house (that was home to Rocky, Stripes, Rosa and Leo), night came – and with it, the usual haunting sounds of the wolves and other creatures of the night.

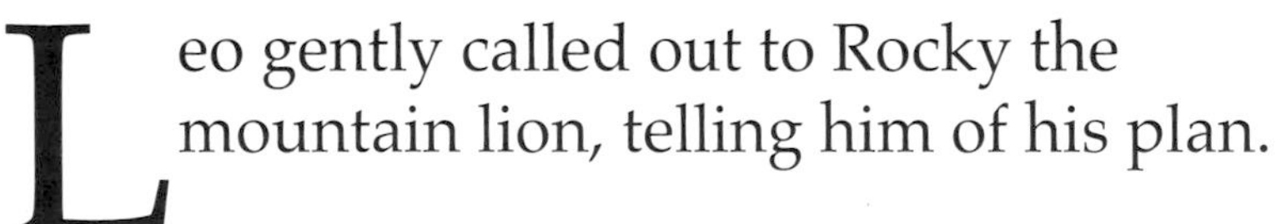

Leo gently called out to Rocky the mountain lion, telling him of his plan.

"You must be joking," cried Rocky. "Escape! Honestly Leo, with talk like that, you're gonna get us transferred to another zoo. I'm sorry cat, but tell it to the paw cos' the face ain't listening."

"Fine, fine, I'll go alone," said Leo.

Just then a deep rumbling voice like a well-oiled motorbike came from next door.

It was Stripes, a beautifully handsome Bengal tiger.

"I am wanting to take the risk for one night of fun and freedom under the night sky," he said.

Rocky, not wanting to be left out, quietly growled, "Okay, okay, count me in Leo."

"But what about Rosa?" Leo replied.

"Sorry she's in the sickbay under quarantine, with a badly swollen paw," answered Stripes.

So, the feline trio discussed how to escape and, with the help of a set of lost keys, an extremely cunning monkey called Fingers and Spectacles the raccoon, it would happen soon.

No sooner had the three cats planned it, than it was time to do it!

Spectacles was right on time after being given the keys by Fingers.

Silently, each of the cat's cages were opened by Spectacles' agile little fingers.

In a flash, the three cats were out and on their way. Freedom at last!

Fresh smells mingled with the midnight air filling their nostrils, and the promise of excitement lay before them. How awesome and majestic they looked as they padded along in single file, silhouetted by the glow of the full moon.

The three cats reached a small clearing in the surrounding forest, where they would be safe from prying eyes. After marking some of the trees with their razor sharp claws, they flopped to the floor. Swiftly rolling onto their backs, Rocky, Stripes and Leo decided to celebrate slipping through the zoo's security system by having a good old scratch.

Gazing up at the faraway stars somehow made them all feel very small.

And for a few minutes, the three cats just lay in wonder.

Stripes broke the silence.

"These stars remind me of home," he said.

His face went a little sad. Stripes began to tell Leo and Rocky how he remembered as a cub crashing through the tall grass, whilst being chased by the hunters who had killed his parents for their beautiful fur coats.

Stripes, seeming a little happier, went on to say how he had been rescued by a kind human who cared for him until it was no longer safe for him to stay, and he was sent here to My Zoo.

Stripes turned to Leo and said, "What about you Leo, and how does a leopard have such a lion-sounding name anyway?"

Leo thought for a while then said, "My ancestors came from Africa but I was born here at My Zoo; it's called being bred in captivity. This is why just being under the stars and moon for one night means so much to me. I can pretend I'm free, roaming the African Savannah, hunting for my own food and raising a family of my own.

"The reason for my lion-sounding name is simple: the granddaughter of the owner of My Zoo couldn't read the word leopard, she kept saying leo-pard, so that's what they called me."

Leo,pard
Leopard: panthera pardus
Bred in captivity

Silence. Then, "Canada, born and bred and proud of it too," snarled Rocky.

"I was shipped over here about four years ago to see a lady friend and start a family, but sadly we couldn't have any cubs. I still remember home very clearly. The mountains, the rivers and the baking hot sun; yep it was sure fine, although at times it was a real struggle to survive. So the zoo's not so bad, especially at feeding times! But to be out here's just swell and if we could do this once in a while, we'd have the best of both worlds."

The three cats all agreed, and with these thoughts decided it was time to sneak back to the zoo, before it started to get light and they were spotted missing. The three cats shook tails and made a pact to repeat their little field trip, but next time Rosa would come along too – bad paw or no bad paw.

As the cats approached the zoo, Leo jumped onto a garden wall much to the surprise of one of their much smaller cousins, a domestic ginger tomcat, who doubled in size at the very sight of them. Poor thing!

Arching over onto the garden wall was a beautiful and highly scented white rose, which Leo snapped off with his very powerful mouth.

Perfect, he thought, this he would give to Rosa.

Once in the grounds of the zoo, the three cats made a slight detour to visit poor Rosa who was in an area not on view to the public.

Leo suddenly had a strange fleeting feeling; something was not quite right.

Rosa was indeed very pleased to see them and hear of their adventures.

Pushing the rose through the wire, it fell beneath her strong, round, muscular face. Rosa immediately sniffed at its sweet aroma and savoured the smells and scents it carried from other creatures outside the zoo.

Suddenly, without warning and as fast as a flash, a small furry creature sprang past them with the agility of an Olympic gymnast and, almost as though its body contained no bones whatsoever, magically squeezed through the small wire openings of Rosa's cage.

The creature, now standing proud and amazingly still after such speed, announced itself.

"It is I, Louis blue-eyes, one of the keepers and protectors of the sacred rose bush. I must stay with the bloom you brought here until it dies, withers, then falls apart."

The four cats could not decide if this tiny little feller was brave, stupid or both, for following them back to the zoo. After better inspection, the three cats soon realised it was indeed the same domestic cat they had taken by surprise and frightened on the garden wall earlier.

Disbelief quickly turned to joy; Rocky, Stripes and Leo-Pard roared and roared with laughter so loudly that they must have woken up some of the night sleepers at the zoo.

Rosa purred with gratitude and said, “What will my keeper think when he finds my beautiful gift and its odd little protector in the morning?” They all agreed it would have him dumbfounded and guessing for weeks, if not years, as to how on earth they had got there.

Rocky, Stripes and Leo quickly hurried off to their own quarters, where they were greeted by Spectacles the raccoon, who was patiently waiting for them with the keys to let them back in.

Spectacles would then hide the keys until the next time they were needed, which hopefully wouldn't be too long.

As for the rose and its protector, the keeper did indeed find them. Gossip grew and spread all over the zoo, drawing attention in the local, then national news.

The newspapers were full of it: "How did they get there?" "A rose for Rosa?" "Did the cat bring it?" "If so why? And if not, then who did?"

THE MOON
VIDEOS

Rosa was by now out of quarantine and she, her rose and her by-now-inseparable little guest were all back in Rosa's usual home. Rosa found it funny as she gazed through half-closed eyes as reporters and photographers bumped into each other in order to get the best pictures of her, Louis blue-eyes, and the now-withered brown but still intact rose.

Rocky, Stripes and Leo just lay there flicking and twitching their tails with a smug look on their faces, knowing their secret was safe with more yet to come!

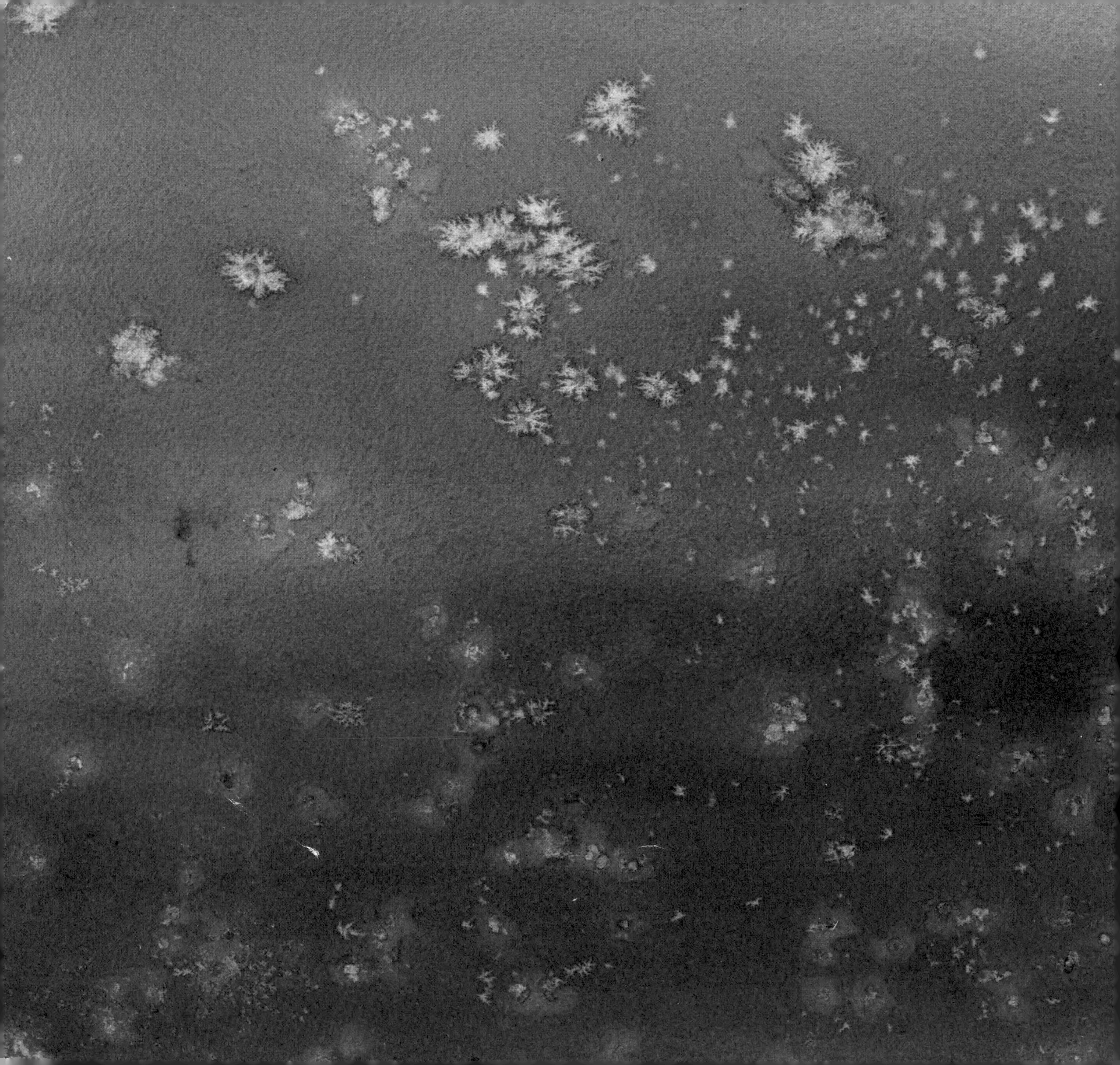

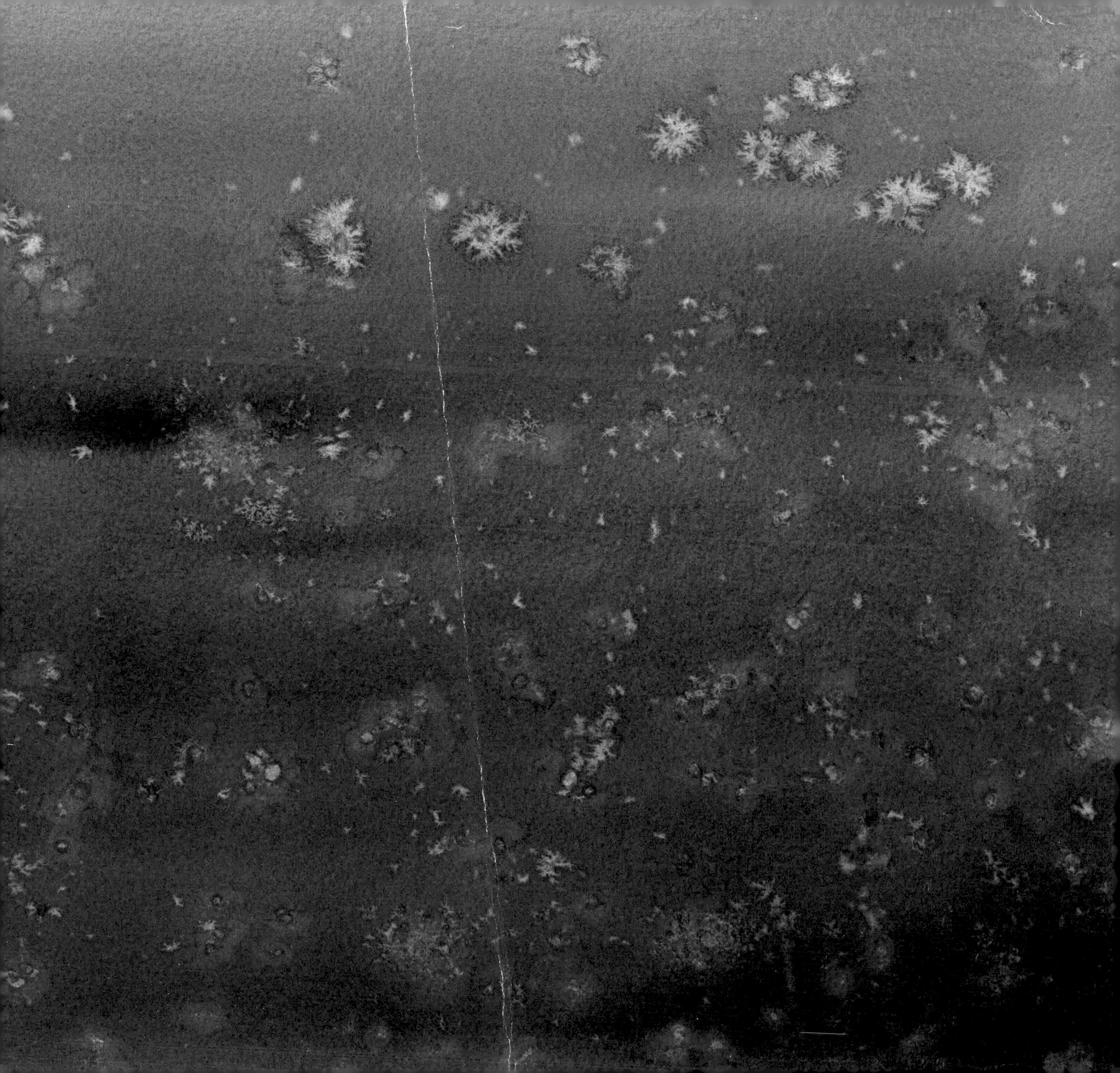